LIVING

First published in 2025 by the Cambridge Queer Press
an imprint of MFco Ltd. Unit 4 City Limits, Danehill, Reading
RG6 4UP, UK.

ISBN 978-1-912622-57-3

Cover image: Enes Akdoğan
https://www.pexels.com/photo/brunette-in-white-shirt-27153650

Text is set in Cormorant Garamond 13pt on 19pt.

LIVING
Tuesday 17th

C. FARR

Cambridge
Queer Press

C. FARR

Little is known about C. Farr except that they live on the east coast of England. They avoid, as far as possible, contact with the outside world. They are fiercely protective of their anonymity.

Their first work for the Cambridge Queer Press was *How To Write Like Mrs Woolf*, an experimental essay-fiction hybrid which explores the methods and characteristics of Virginia Woolf's most innovative prose.

The present volume, *Tuesday 17th*, is the first instalment of a vast multi-part work, *Living*, intended to evoke the chaotic and unstructured narrative of a whole life, as lived.

C. Farr has described the endeavour as "life from writing rather than writing from life".

The second installment *November 2nd* will by published by the Cambridge Queer Press as part of our Autumn List 2026.

*ALEKSANDRA
POGOSSKAIA*

Where does one begin with a writer like C. Farr? So little is known about the person or the circumstances that stand behind the creation of the mammoth work, *Living*.

All we know for certain is that C. Farr is a determined recluse and a condition of publication is that no further details about their life may be divulged. Farr asks, not unreasonably, that the writing speaks for itself.

This is the first glimpse, then, of a very large text. There are an estimated one million words of extant manuscript in service to the idea of "writing life" so that it unfolds as a vivified, breathing and twitching thing.

The intention that moves behind the enormous manuscript of *Living* is "life from writing not writing from life". Like Baron von Frankenstein, C. Farr aims to create life anew (not with electricity but at the cost of a million words, if necessary). This is a very different proposition from the biographer or memoirist who "writes a life". With an enormous and unruly river of words, Farr brings life into being with all its bloodiness, vagaries, faults, spare parts, retraced steps, mixed-up brains, and maddening inconsistencies.

Life is imperfect of course, boring sometimes, confusing often. We contradict ourselves, move around, fall over, fall in and out of love, lose our way. The text, unspared, is made to do the same.

Living is a beast of a manuscript, which is both its failing and its triumph. No part of the text appears planned or particularly structured – at least on first reading. Its free form gives rise to a life as unpredictable, uncontrollable, visceral and troubling as von Frankenstein's pot-luck monster. Farr deliberately eschews conventional narrative order. All of life is here in a great jumble for better or worse and one of the major editorial challenges is not to neaten or "gussy up" the text too much. *It lives! It lives!*

A minimal amount of editorial intervention is necessary, however, to enable the average reader to find their way into the text. The editor must answer the author's demands for fidelity to the intention behind *Living* and at the same time meet the needs of a general reading public. It would be a dereliction of editorial duty to offer too few footholds on the one hand or, at the other extreme, to err too far on the side of providing "literary form". It can be argued that the imposition of form for form's sake would undermine or defeat the author's aims entirely.

Famously, the Danish philosopher Kierkegaard noted, "Life can only be understood backwards but it must be lived forwards." No life is edited or footnoted. Life-as-lived offers none of these textual luxuries. Farr's writing pursues that difficult-to-fathom forward-only journey at all costs. It is as if Farr, like us, has no choice but to press on in the absence of hindsight.

So much of life is often misread. Why should Farr's text be any different? It is only after the event and with maturity that life's hurriedly-cobbled-together, tangled strands can be separated and interpreted.

Wilfully erratic, Farr's text is often very beautiful, too. Much of that beauty derives from its quixotic, peripatetic point of view. The text is constantly in motion. That Farr has written "poetic prose" can be a condemnation rather than a commendation. Most examples of poetic prose are disastrous. There are very few exceptions: Elizabeth Smart's *By Grand Central Station I Sat Down and Wept* (1945) may be one but it, too, has its detractors. A truer and fairer comparison might be with the writing of the English painter and author Denton Welch (29 March 1915 – 30 December 1948). In Welch's texts, the minutest details of experience are evoked by meticulous – and lovely – description. It is as if Welch has his nose pressed up against the surface of life and sees everything, describes everything with a corresponding intensity; it is hallucinatory rather than chaotic but it is kin to C. Farr's prose.

Welch/Farr are unafraid of the mundanity of life, and they are unafraid of evoking both that mundanity and life's miraculousness in the same breath. This is how their texts avoid the pitfalls of most poetic prose; they are never sanctimonious, sentimental, or "purple" because they give the reader life "warts and all".

Whilst Farr's text is often contradictory, oscillating from place to place, time to time, changing time, remarking on the pliability of time, there is an organising thought that underlies and scaffolds this first volume. The writer P.D. Ouspensky (referenced unequivocally in the text) contended that it is entirely possible to be born, live and die without development of the self, without fulfilling one's potential as a human being. In this scenario, the entity that was the individual simply passes away irretrievably.

But there is another possibility: the individual may consciously aim to develop their understanding. They may struggle to become fully realised and, in this conscious self-development, give rise to something that does not pass away irretrievably but which has a sustained and enduring existence across the wastes of time.

These ideas of development and non-development stand at the heart of *November 17th*.

Its inner organisation serves the exploration of Ouspenskian thought, which in turn provides the outer raison d'etre of the work. Accordingly, the idea of "making something of oneself" recurs throughout the text.

Notably, a psalm on the radio is misheard. Farr's text provides an accurate record of the mishearing in which the sense of the original is entirely lost (the lines are gibberish) but something else emerges from the garbled language, some abstracted sense of the grandeur of the original. We do not know "what happened" in a literal sense but we know "what we feel" as a result of the misheard psalm. Something is made of the mis-hearing; the narrative is faulty but the living, moving, quality of it is without peer.

November 17th is a love story between the narrator, presumably C. Farr (though there may be dangers in making that assumption) and a lovely young "resting" actor called Simon. The events described are both a lunch shared in a swanky London restaurant and a literary/artistic experiment in which the narrator experiments with "writing out life for us". The strangest aspect of the narrative is that it is both life being lived as something unknowable, in forward motion, unfolding; and an experiment in writing out possible scenarios for life before it has been lived. The experiment consists of writing out possible futures and then "living into" the writing until one of the possible narratives triumphs as the most viable for the protagonists – "which version will be gifted to reality" as C. Farr expresses it.

The French novelist, Marguerite Duras (4 April 1914 – 3 March 1996) appears in the text as writer, muse and committed alcoholic. Her presence indicates Farr's familiary with the *Nouvelle Roman* of the 1950s and 60s and its preoccupation with subjective experience, individual perception, and language itself, rather than plot or character development. We can see a complex, reflexive relationship between *November 17th* and the work of Duras. Both are real and actual, fictional and provisional. Farr echoes Durassian prose, as if dancing with her words, on more than one occasion. This is Duras in *The Lover*

(1984): "Years after the war, after marriages, children, divorces, books, he came to Paris with his wife."

This is Farr in *November 17th*: "You can still conjure Simon all these years later after wars, economic crises, divorces…"

The reservation for the fateful lunchtime rendezvous is made in the name of "Lol Stein", a reference to Duras's novel *Le ravissement de Lol V. Stein/The Ravishing of Lol Stein*: "She had lived her early years as though she were waiting for something she might, but never did, become."

Duras described herself as "a real writer and a real alcoholic" and Farr does not shy away from conceding the benefits of alcohol to the writer. Alcohol frees the writing hand to work from a place of uncensored feeling. And alcohol provides enabling Dutch courage to the protagonist of *November 17th*:

"And how profound is the effect of a glass of red wine; the second glass even more so. If you do not drink, you shrink from the enemy but a vodka martini from the bar – transparent, pure, concentrate – has the effect of a half-bottle of wine in one small violently cold glass. You were changed so suddenly, so instantaneously that the change had already occurred before you were aware of it.

"You discovered this kinship with alcohol a long time ago but still it catches you by surprise every time."

It seems safe to say that Farr was/is aware of the potential for precocity in all this. Of the young actor, Simon, Farr writes: "The cords in his throat caught in the lamplight like columns supporting a pediment. He is Dali's *Self Portrait with Raphaelesque Neck*." The portrait in question, by the Surrealist Salvador Dali, is a work of juvenilia more than a little tinged with self-aggrandisement. Farr seems to be acknowledging that this first volume is similarly situated in juvenilia, is similarly and knowingly and necessarily overcooked.

Revelation in one form or another recurs throughout Farr's text. One thing is ripped away from another, often without rhyme or reason.

Youth is constantly surprised by things newly seen that the rest of us would simply take for granted. Things are stripped bare, seen directly and clearly as opposed to being hidden by propriety.

Same sex relationships were illegal in Britain until 1967 and, even then, the Sexual Offences Act of that year only partially decriminalised gay sex under certain circumstances in England and Wales. C. Farr is all too aware that some things are difficult or dangerous to reveal. Farr knows that truth may come with a cost.

Revelation takes place, necessarily, in the stream of time which is, itself, an unreliable phenomenon in *November 17th*. The title *November 17th* is redolent of a given point in time but it is so unspecific as to be almost meaningless. Time is not the tyrant we think it is. Time elongates or curtails itself, just to keep us on our toes. "The watched pot never boils." "Time flies when you're having fun." Farr-time slows and speeds up, flexes, surprises, dismays, separates and brings together. It also prompts nostalgia for time past, for things that are lost and irretrievable.

Loss finds its counterbalance in the idea of "looking forward". This sounds like a choice but is simply our fate. In one instance, the protagonist looks forward to the high tower of Salle church. It is first glimpsed in the distance as if it were "a piece of missing information". The protagonist arrives at the church – at the thing anticipated – and this new proximity is equated with proximity to knowledge. What might seem a long way off is perhaps present and actual all along. Everything you need to know may be already to hand. Time may be a loop, not a line.

Early on, *November 17th* sets out Farr's stall in relation writing as an art form. Farr tells us one must be in service to art wholeheartedly; one must know it leads to something of value, but also realise that the value of any work is independent of money and reputation. After a night at the opera, the conversation turns to the idea that the artist must "shake the snowstorm of life". There must be a roughness or abrasiveness to the art if it is to be art at all. A great painting may be ugly. It may need to be ugly to be great. For anything to be art not artifice, it must be ennobled by flaw. The flaws in C. Farr's text are like the flaws added intentionally to a Persian carpet so as not to offend God, the sole purveyor of perfection.

Oblique but significant references are made to alternative techniques of composition: Gertrude Stein's "continuous present"; the composer Erik Satie's rejection of 19th-century Romanticism and his focus on simplicity and repetition; and Arnold Schoenberg's twelve-tone technique. These references, though fleeting, suggest Farr, too, is working out a new compositional technique, a new way of organising language and narrative, the better to capture the experience of living in the unfolding moment.

Winter arrives in the opening pages; both an end and a beginning. Farr's winter is like Virginia Woolf's frost fair in *Orlando* – outrageously, preternaturally cold. Pheasants are frozen into folds in the earth. Everything is petrified, waiting for the thaw. This is a terrific metaphor for the text itself, something just starting to come to life, the first 10,000 words of the 990,000 words still to follow. Winter seizes and dominates the landscape. "The landscape caught in the grip of something not altogether nice..." This not altogether nice thing turns out to be Christmas. Along the way we encounter paganism, witchcraft and feasting in the dark. There is a whiff of anti-clericalism in the air, a resentment that Johnny-cum-lately Christianity has co-opted the much older, indigenous festival of Yule. Nothing is quite one thing or another, though. As in life, things are neither black nor white.

Paris appears as itself, the capital of France, and as the "Fictional City of Paris", a kind of Weil-esque *City of Mahagonny* brimming with political intrigue, love and song. It is a fictional city and the romance enacted in it is similarly a fiction. The protagonist is "writing up" the lovers' lunchtime rendezvous, giving it a certain kind of life as fiction first and then attempting to live into it as written. The question becomes, which of these fictional possibilities will solidify as lived reality? As the French existentialists noted, "One choice is the death of all other choices." You cannot spend spring on the French Riviera *and* in the Swiss Alps. One must deny the other.

This brings us neatly back to C. Farr's insistence on "creating life from writing not writing from life". First it must be written up from whatever stray fragments the writer can lay hands on. It is written first by Farr and then enacted by a cast who have not yet seen the script. What results is life, bloodied and bandaged and staggering about, just as Baron von Frankenstein would recognise it:

"You tell me you are waiting for something to be revealed. I tell you I have written all this already. I have written into life and you must read it. But I say the revelation, if there is to be one, must come from you. I can't do it all by myself. You made the Seine gunmetal, beautiful; there was nothing of me in it. You made the café alive with temperament. There was nothing of me in any of it. I was incapable of reaction without you. I could act only under your tutelage."

Pogosskaia / Cambridge 2025

LIVING

And when you add it all up,
this is what our lives will have been,
an accumulation of small,
seemingly unimportant choices.

TUESDAY *17th*

Gertrude Stein lived at 20 Gordon Square when she was a young woman.[1] London wasn't for her – too damp and too dirty. You have to be born to London. Sit in the Duveen Room at the British Museum at lunchtime and contemplate the Elgin marbles.[2] Go for the room; the height and soft grey hush of it. Sit and imagine yourself free. And after a little while, you can go back to real life and the business of earning a living, and it doesn't seem so bad. London becomes something in the Autumn. Wander around Gordon Square when the rain's coming down. The spent leaves fill the gutters up with gold.

Somewhere between Long Acre and Seven Dials, an unmarked door, a deep racing green colour. The door thrown back and an astonishing welcome from a Spaniard (you have never met before) in a dark blue v-neck jumper. The business of shaking hands; bags to be put away; coats hung. And then into the little dining room with white linens and a white glass screen so the hoi polloi can't peer into the dining room from the street. A theatre club, very quiet this early in the day, full of thinnish light from the misty glass and the white table cloths. A dish of pale golden olive oil, some italian bread. Everything white – linen, plates – everything a wan monochrome but for the pool of yellow oil.

Now the reason for your visit: Gareth. The sudden turn in the conversation to the wish for recognition. O yes we want to be recognised for what we do. We want our struggles to be marked by affection, respect. We want the ease of a certain kind of living. But if you pursue recognition for its own sake, there will always be someone more recognised than you. Only if you live most intensely in your own living are you without rival.

It ought to be enough to be admired by the good and the dear and the clear-headed but always there's the desire for public acclaim, or rather, for the legitimacy that would suggest. Feeling this less so many years later perhaps; now the desire instead for a certain kind of living.

"Thank you, George" for the salt and pepper; George, with out-sized reynard moustache and equally out-sized pepper mill spilling black snow. Before today, Gareth had seemed so fantastically charismatic, so confident. It had been impossible to guess he was so under-baked inside.

Espresso to finish in the little basement sitting room – rickety chairs; lumpy, mean cushions. Then the march back up to Seven Dials, Cambridge Circus, Charing Cross Road, feeling wistful because of the wine; full of love for life, people, the impossible work of writing; the fuming and thundering traffic; the greasy pavements. Walk and reflect. After any discovery there is always a hollow feeling like the backwash from a spent wave. Ask yourself, where does living lead now? There is always, at least, the desire to make something of ourselves. You just had lunch at *Peg's Club* with a paper-skinned man. Not knowing people this wonderful existed — with skin as thin as the skin of an onion.

That wet Tuesday afternoon, the medievalism of the road menders repairing the cobbles in Monmouth Street with an iron rod.[3] An odd feeling of lost grandeur, or lost relevance. An echo in the memory of the white-coated waiters, the dining room; George dropping the pepper mill. The conversation about fear pressing down. And yes we are all probably fearful. So we retreat, steel ourselves against life, modify our ambitions.

Later at home, words from a canticle on the radio: "Show thyself!" You hope to discover yourself – whatever that means – which involves the risk of sailing over the edge of the world.

Later still, two suns: one in the canal at Little Venice and one low in the sky. A double blinding. You steal time for yourself in the café on the canal. Perhaps you have an idea of where you want to go but you have no idea how to get there. You need people, thought, letters; how helpful letters have been to clear the mind, find the root or rock under the idea; not an idea simply made up but one struggled with together, realised between you. You think to yourself, We'll just muddle along, perplex ourselves, and from the general chaos something will arise. We would prefer a system, a guaranteed way of going on but there is no certainty of course. Or there is the *only* certainty.

You've waited so long for the stolen hour in the café, when it finally comes, you're unable to write, dried up, empty, afraid. You're afraid of living up to yourself. You have to have a disengaged faith that at the end *lies* something. The café is a good place to be. Now you understand Hemingway in Paris.[4] We all need a home to go to. *What good is sitting alone in your room*, Sally Bowles? Isherwood gave her the name because he was in love with composer Paul Bowles – home in Tangiers; the sky of north Africa, sheltering men like those.[5]

Sit here in the warm of the café, then. The dying sun, pictures on the walls – of figures, darkly drawn. The smell of coffee, cigarette smoke. Foreign voices. A piano accordion. The whole thing may be fake but the warmth and the hum of voices are real enough. The sun has set while you've sat here. Time seems to have drawn itself out, like a piece of toyed-with chewing gum; out, out. You're interested in the business of swapping lives. You can have mine if I can try yours. Has it ever occurred to you how the smallest thing, missed by everyone else, may be the source of the most astonishing change?

You think of holidays: Sicily, Cambridge, Norfolk. A wave, an ocean breaker of lavender. And the heat in the valley like a blow to the head. You were able to think at a stretch on holiday. Gertrude Stein said that paragraphs were emotional and sentences were not — or vice versa. But what does that really mean?[6]

The golden oil in a little dish at *Peg's Club*. Gold on white. The road to lucidity is stony. I am only at the beginning. But I have begun. Marguerite Duras said of her alcoholism, "I drank because I was an alcoholic. I was a real one – like a writer. I'm a real writer, I was a real alcoholic. I drank red wine to fall asleep. Afterwards, Cognac in the night. Every hour a glass of wine and in the morning Cognac after coffee, and afterwards I wrote." And, "In the American hospital, while I was in a coma, I had lucid intervals." You had an idea of yourself as a writer and worked to fulfil that idea (until very recently you believed a greater understanding would express itself in a renewed language). Remake language to give the whole sense without error or distortion. Language does not connect but divides us. A variety of acer is a forest of hands. On the chest, a basket of oranges and lemons with the sun on it. Outside, the sun lowering behind the cow parsley, everything light-filled, three-dimensional. But "a basket of oranges with the sun on it" doesn't give it; and the day doesn't live again.[7] Kierkegaard said it, "What an abyss of uncertainty, whenever the mind feels overtaken by itself: when it, the seeker, is at the same time the dark region through which it must go seeking?" Somewhere along the way, you managed to lose faith in the English language itself. The imperative to write is different, modified now. It is living that is so intoxicating and real and moving. What a mess!

Later, huddled over the stove in Norfolk, staring through the little window at the dull red coals, the growing heart;[8] a little box of condensed heat. Cold at your back. A glass of viciously cold champagne; culpable to drink it so cold.[9] A head full of nothing. There cannot be money in it or recognition in it. It's not even certain what it is. But you do have faith that it does lead somewhere very slowly, with difficulty perhaps, but it does lead somewhere.

Do not speak now except for the sake of friends and the effect of their listening — you hear yourself more clearly that way. Is there enough courage in you for your work to be nothing, a ringing silence, an open space?

Everything returns to absences and intervals.

The strange intimacy it's possible to feel with people you hardly know. Arriving here, to the room with the stove, very late. Incredible cold. A barn owl hunting the verge like a soft, silent light in the sky. The Norfolk house frozen inside. Devastating tiredness. A lovely little book turned suddenly, shockingly erotic. Except nothing shocks you but cruelty. The little sitting room alive with colour and the gathering heat. Stardust from the devastating effects of the cold. If you are young enough, but not too young; if your home is in London so you are not defeated by that city; if you are young and ambitious and live in that city towards the end of the 20th Century, then you can count yourself more fortunate than almost anyone else alive.[10]

You do not want to sleep just yet. Your whole body hunched over the little safe of the stove. Peering in at what? Lost in what? In the extremity of exhaustion, cold, the sudden bolting effect of the wine.

Next day: high winter. Brittle sun. Stunned landscape. Turned earth frosted all day. The sun did nothing to warm away the frost; partridges stuck down, plastered between the white furrows. A day of buying: warm coats and dressing gowns, 2 large bears from eastern Europe, pictures; a curious picture of French tarts, soldiers and an odd figure in the background running forwards, everyone's clothes strangely matching.

And from the dealer, Anthony, a porcelain

Pierrot embracing his Columbine in her yellow gown, both Pierrot and Columbine's shoulders pierced through, with cavities below to hold water for flowers. Anthony, a lovely golden, freckly colour because he has been to Gran Canaria.

Lunch of smoked salmon baguettes; the bread just out of the oven, hot and crisp, damp and doughy inside.

And now it's dark again. Just like that. Nose running. The need to be alone because alone has a variety of freedom and spontaneity about it. Alone but surrounded by people, writing surrounded by people. Something will show itself. You want to be recognised for what you do but you don't want to do anything for the sake of being recognised. Far beyond the desire for recognition, your immediate joy in living. Throw off a hundred skins. How little actually matters. How much is self-absorption. Throw it all away.

Yesterday: serious snow. The long slow drive back to London with the serious snow beating at the windscreen and the road grooved with ice.

Perhaps it is because you have a cold but you

feel apathetic, unmoved to move. Then full up of coffee, energised like Alice B. Toklas,[11] buzzing with coffee, putting yourself in the safe hands of Gertrude Stein. Until there was only the oil in the little dish at Peg's Club, only the thin gold of the oil in its white dish; white cloth, white light, white walls; a kind of white omission, a white non-ism with the pale yellow oil at its centre.

Later still, throwing back the door to find Soviet Katya in an extravagant hat! Katya whose first impression of London was grass – grass everywhere. (She had grown up in the snow-bound centre of Russia.) Katya who escaped the collapsing USSR to play and teach piano in England, to marry, to have a child. (But all that comes much later.) A great success of a hat like an inverted, brimmed flowerpot. The new look, new all over again.

In a furnished room in Westbourne Park Katya sings gypsy songs at the piano. Gypsy songs after Brahms and before Debussy. And all this will be lost. Chaos will engulf us. Our creative energy – to make our lives, our work, our relationships –

will flow, weaken and be lost. That will have been that. To have felt so much so deeply and for nothing of it to remain.

Then Katya says, "You have lit a light inside me. And now it burns there."

Perhaps the thing sought is netted in the search itself. Perhaps the thing *is* the search and the question is the answer. So close.[12]

That feeling from all those years ago, something connected with the countryside, Walton,[13] a naïveté, a sort of "freshness of hope". (Is that the best expression you can manage?) Is it significant that the feeling should return now? Perhaps it is to do with being on the edge of something new. And the hope is the hope of imminent discovery.

The strangest dream: I am at an airport. Coffee in a café. I leave my passport on the table. When I try to check-in, there is the problem of the missing passport. A "fix-it" man runs off to retrieve it. Everyone is ready to leave but me. When I regain the passport, the woman at check-in insists on showing me maps of China, provinces, temples... I didn't even know I was travelling to China; just over it, I thought. And when I finally dash aboard, it is not an aeroplane but a French saloon car, a *Leon Bollée*,[14] very crowded with people. I ask when do we get to the aeroplane? And the others in the car laugh and say, "O no, we go all the way in the *Leon Bollée*." There is a strange cubicle, a sort of half bathroom. And one of the women laughs crudely about seeing and hearing everyone "go". I say, "I don't want to sit in this car. I don't want this." I get out in the pouring rain and laugh as the car speeds off. I tell myself I don't need the *Leon Bollée* or the trip to China.

The dark months before Christmas. Rusted hedges. Rain like dirty jewels at the windows. The struggle to be warm. Suddenly everything is enchanted again, as if newly seen and heard. Wide blank skies; Edith Sitwell's "goose weather".[15] Wanting to be outside in the light and air and, after a very short time, the reverse desire to be back inside by the stove, muffled up against the cold and dark. The landscape caught in the grip of something not altogether nice; superstition, witchery; and the whole lot rolling up towards Christmas, to the doors of the Parish churches.[16] The sudden "glory in the dark" of Christmas, like a bauble, insane hope lighting up the darkest day of the year. Nostalgia for a time passed, for an atmosphere, a spirit in the air so many years ago. To be happy in the moment, caught up in the spirit and romance of the moment that extends back and forth interminably. Something is about to be made known to you – a vital piece of information. Perhaps it is always close by, just at your elbow. Every need met. The extraordinary feeling of quiet, benevolent conspiracy. There was singing in the square; the first chords of something. And suddenly, stepping out into the light, you saw trestle tables, charming nonsense laid out, treasure. The melancholic effect of broken china (a *Limoges* hot chocolate cup with a broken handle and a wire-stitched lid, loved, battered, repaired, finally given up on). Pressed glass candlesticks, a picture of Emmanuel College, Cambridge.

Then supper together with – let's not name the culprit. Enough to know we were already old, already too long married. A chicken pot-roasted. Mashed potatoes. The tail end of your cold, a horrible dismaying cold. The warmth of the stove heating both storeys at the south gable. Sewing, listening to the radio, the piano, writing in French. Rain outside, mist at the windows, a thousand litres of heating oil in the tank and the air hard to breath because it is laden with frost.

And at Reepham, a tall fir dressed in white lights, the rain coming out of a midnight blue sky. Depth and darkness and the eternity of mud. The temporariness of one, the twofold temporariness of two. Keep your treasures close. Appreciate all that you have, they say. Life is here and you are living. Love – the genuine article – is sedate. You want to be held by something exquisite. Unspoken. Felt at the lowest point, like the rubbing of a double bass, or some other low-toned instrument.

The dark is extraordinary now. So little of the waking day is lit. Shopping in the dark. Buying bread and eggs and red wine and placing the bags by touch inside the car. All day, the long slow fade to dark; frozen earth; yellow light at the windows – the life of houses, the long slow eternal rhythm of the life of a house. And perhaps the people come and go but the life of the house is uninterruptable.

Out into the flat open heart of Norfolk. The road twists without obstacles; merely the corner of this field, or that. And the sudden leaping up, beating up into the air of a startled barn owl, white against the limitless, lightless sky. Rain is falling. A slumped, blanket sky. The darkly pinnacled tower of Salle church,[17] far in the distance. Piano – Satie[18] – on the car radio. Look too far into the distance, and you've missed the thing at your feet. Steam on the windscreen. The slow roll of the landscape as the car makes equally slow progress. The high-up rolls and sudden folds in the landscape, poplars folded away, lowered into deep folds in the earth.

Looking for something or desiring something which is, perhaps, already there.

At last: the enormous church at Salle with its four-ton crowns. The flat landscape flatter than the sea. Hedges torn up. The great descent into something. The land open just as far as the dark line of the horizon. The wind getting up. Always rain at this time of year. The magic hours between 3.30 and 5.30pm. The rare, special, dark hours.

Sitting inside as the dark comes down and the wind is up and it is so cold in the house despite the heating. Writing in outdoor coats. Tomorrow will be one of those rare days when it's possible to be inside all day.

Later, back in London, breakfast on the canal with Louise. "More detail here about Louise," the editor at the Cambridge Queer Press requests.[19] But I cannot remember anything about her other than her name. Very little occurs when we're together but somehow things get done. I tell Louise that the work always leaps ahead, finds a way ahead after we've met, which makes her sound important. But she is lost, absolutely, to the past.

Walking by the canal in the half light. Buy

food. A chicken. Sour cream. Red wine. To make "Gypsy Goulash", an Alice Toklas recipe.[20] Gypsy goulash for Thursday with Russian pianist Katya and beloved Simon, the gardener's help, pale as a lily and twice as lovely. The goulash is a hit and so is our little triumvirate: pianist, actor/gardener, artist. We drink too much, talk too much, think everything we say has a brilliant originality and importance to it when all we really are is young.

That tall fir decorated with white lights in the square at Reepham; rain tumbling and the white-lit fir, and all around the little market town, the landscape, peeling back like the flat rectangular lid of a sardine tin. You can look for something and see it as being necessarily outside, impossibly far away from you. Then it's almost inevitable that you discover the thing looked for has been close to hand all along. This is living. Suddenly everything is drawn in, pulled up close. All the places you have ever visited, all the things you have ever seen, all the words you have ever said have a life inside you, consciously or unconsciously in a parallel and unending "now".[21]

The enigma of Louise and her "Caroline shoes". I remember these were shoes hoped for and pleaded for as a child. "Caroline shoes" because of the effect of the shoes, like the transforming, glorifying effect of that name, *Caroline*, in the mind of the child, Louise. The shoes are all I can remember now. The only thing left. At least I tried. Your life is that row of tin lids, rectangular, smooth, pulled back, perfectly bright. After the first flush of ambition, after emulating others you admire, you let go of all that. The lid is turned back on itself.

Walking across the Stody Estate, perhaps ten miles from the sea. Life used to feel ordinary and now it feels charmed, shone up. A rather blank, water-filled sky. Walking high up over the countryside. Now the grey box of Hunworth Church in the sudden quiet. Christmas over. Visitors departed. The departing hoped for and now regretted. Sad, quiet, thin time, alone. The house and life gone. To work, to write is impossible in the thick of life. Only afterwards, and only with hindsight.

Later, my friend Stéphane said, "You are the only one to have the courage to write this *manifest*." Well yes, Stéphane! You are onto something about courage and making. My desk faces the wall not the window. Whatever occurs doesn't occur out there.

An afternoon with Jenny at the Middlesex Hospital (my friend Jenny Cole has written a book called *Journeys with a Cancer*), then a trip to HMV to buy some kind of compensation. A boxed set of Shoenberg. Wanting to be confronted by twelve-tone, something at the edge of things for its own sake; something for the sake of learning, of having better tools for the job we are trying to do.[22]

Or coffee at Patisserie Valerie in Marylebone High Street. Stephen Berkoff at the next table. No word from Simon, the gardener's help, lily-lovely and apparently just as rare. No lunch, no card, no note. You have to decide how you feel about that. Is he thoughtless? Or is he just young?

That night, the Opera House was full of

painted monsters. Not quite grotesque; you'd have had some redeeming feeling for the grotesque. No, these were mediocre monsters, clinging on to a misjudged propriety, which was simply a certain kind of ignorance behind a certain kind of competence. They lacked the courage to be frankly grotesque. And it's there in the language – gruesome not grotesque. Grotesque would have been gothic, emphatic, admirable, enough to "shake the snowstorm" of life.

Tosca and the magic of the *Te Deum*. Good and evil. Scarpia's evil is pitched against the lovers.[(23)] Yes, it's obvious. But that doesn't make it any less true. The high churchy-ness of it all; the incense and the procession and the choir and the bells of the cathedral. You are convinced there's something encoded in religious music, something far more sublime than any religious doctrine. To be at the height of our powers in a great capital city. Talking, laughing, arguing, and Katya always gives you heart because of her beautiful and grave commitment to music, to art.

After the opera, you ate oysters and drank

champagne and stayed up very, very late, talking about the Russian soprano with a heavy, fruity weight in her voice; the importance of its rawness because, according to Katya, the artist must *shake the snowstorm*; there must be some kind of agitation or there will be no effect at all. If everything is smooth, immaculately given, there is no art, only execution. The bright cavern of the brasserie; the scraping of chairs, knives, voices; the waiters asking, how are you since we saw you last? (You go too often.) The champagne is diabolically cold. The oysters are like the breath of the sea. The sudden bolting effect of the champagne; the conversation, unsentimental and unafraid to oppose. The need for some kind of provocation, the need to shake ourselves up. You drank the champagne and shook the snowstorm, and Katya asked questions about your work. And in her very Soviet way, she answered herself before you could: *Yes I think this is a very helpful way of thinking about it and it will open up new ways of working for you.*

All through the opera you knew you would try to write about it afterwards. But whenever you've tried in the past it's been impossible – all that's ever resulted is mawkishness. There is always the problem of *Tosca's* popularity. The "tawdry shocker" as the critic said. But the truth is, you found it ravishing. Sitting at the back of the stalls circle, you saw everything set back, framed by the dark mass of the grand tier above you, the stage resembling an opened box with colour and light and people inside.

Look at the broken cup on your desk. Lift the lid and read inside *Paris-Limoges*, and see if you don't find yourself weeping. That can't be right can it? *Paris Limoges!* O but the wet streets and shuttered cafés and the opening bars of *Suite Bergamasque* and Gertrude Stein and Alice Toklas. All appear briefly. And all that feeling; ambition. But no, that's not it. That's an explanation after the fact. It's just the thought of one of the world's great cities, Paris or London. Riding the tube, there were signal problems and announcements to help people find their way home. So much poetry in the secular litany: *Marylebone, Baker Street, Great Portland Street, Euston Square, Kings*

Cross St. Pancras, Farringdon, Barbican, Moorgate, Liverpool Street. London's own shipping forecast. Something connected with identity.

Simon is always too knowing for his years. Just as you were described, all those years ago, as too knowing for your years. The curious mixture of wit, brightness, and naïveté. You see your own naïveté reprised in a way.

The thing with least dilution from the intention is the prize. Closest to the source, the origin, the first thinking. Closest to the source and so at its most intense and also its most unknown, most unseeable. Strongest, strangest, most vigorous, most unquantifiable, most difficult, least dilute. Something created, made with the hands; appreciating the close texture of life as something consciously and conscientiously well made.[24] You are the whole world. Forgetting. Insulating. Wrapped. The impossibility of hearing anything – your name called (that simple thing your name), a car, a plane, the end of the world – the impossibility of hearing anything above the torrential fall of the sea.

The weekly fleeing to Norfolk. So exhausted the eye becomes lazy. The mind is stunned so it can't calculate properly. Moments of connection so true, it's like pressing your palm flat on a tabletop. True like the fact of dust. The ruthless frost bursts the cells of plants, blackens potatoes frozen into the ground. Then the fog, lying high up at first, and all the lights in the villages blown wide open, haloed, magnified. Notes to self, a kind of stock-taking. You wrote to re-enchant life. A sudden light in the sky. A billion stars visible and frost heavy on the verges and in the trees. And then the light, like the light of a helicopter or a military plane except it is too bright, too big. Breaking up suddenly, its brilliance crumbling away behind it like a passing thought. And then the whole thing goes out, disappears from the sky leaving only the billion stars and the silence and the cold. You, yourself, disappeared from the world – almost from life – for three years. And when you re-entered life, life had become something different while you were away. And the tragedy of Katya saying mightn't you put your insight into a character rather than writing about yourself? All that work, all that effort to step away from that kind of narrative, to step into yourself, to find yourself sufficient; all of that so painfully won.

A madonna at the far end of the harbour facing out to sea. *Stella Maris.* The identity of the port bound up with the little fleet of inshore trawlers. The old harbour with the civic hall and new promenade and modern church because the old one was razed by war. The boats return, draw up to the quays and turn into their moorings. White prows on blue water. The two boats return together, turn together in a trawlerman's *pas de deux.* And you start to see the very great importance of the way things are placed in relation to each other.[25]

Waking up this morning to the sun, hidden somewhere or other in the East, rising slowly, burning off the fallen cloud; frost glittering on the lawn. The barometer rising. Duck eggs into a basin for scrambled duck eggs. And the memory bubbles up, like bubbles rising in a pan of boiling water,[26] of an artifical hen's egg owned by I no longer remember who; all the promise of an egg but a plaster-of-paris deception to make hens broody.

Later, the sun hard on the water, reaching under the surface of the sea, lighting the smooth mud wall. Already your flesh tastes of salt because the wind is rising off the sea. You feel the sea deep underneath you. You feel the weight of it moving. You are on its back.

The shop assistant was humourless. You wanted so much for her to smile and that communicated itself in some way, crossed over from you to her. She hadn't realised this singular transmission, this strange thing had happened. Then she looked up and saw it; perhaps you were weeping. She smiled, startled into it. And you were startled, too, because so fierce had been your sudden love for her.

After that, you realised you were not alone there on the inside. Something else was there with you. Some might go so far as to give it the name "holy ghost".

Christmas is done.

Back to the Shoenberg and the lovely afternoon with Jenny at the Middlesex hospital — meeting her friends Rex and Stan.

Then at the Basil Street Hotel with the mysterious Louise and the paper-skinned Gareth again. Gareth so nervous, as always, looking around for an answer he cannot possibly find outside himself and Louise saying she found it difficult to be with both of us at the same time. You liked Louise for that, for saying these difficult things.

Jenny 48, Jenny's Rex in his 60s, Stan in his 70s; the complexity and confidence of these people, survivors of the revolution, the summer of love, the counterculture, the Vietnam war, flowers, soldiers, guns, flower power. Comparing this afternoon with an afternoon with Simon – all very immediate, quick, energetic, yes; but naïve, brave, foolish, brittle. Of course youth is beguiling because we can't go back; but nor are the young guaranteed the going forward. And yes you can forgive Simon anything just for being Simon; the long cords in his neck; his hands. The cords in his throat caught in the lamplight like columns supporting a pediment.

He is Dali's *Self Portrait with Raphaelesque Neck*.[27] He does what he can. We all do what we can.

You've grown pale. People comment on it, say you're not eating enough or you should drink a glass of red wine for the sake of your blood. Of course you're pale; all of the colour has leached out of your skin. You're bleached, transfigured.

Think of a title, something like *The Fictional City of Paris*: you go to Paris with Simon; eventually they do go to Paris. And it is awful of course. When they go to Paris there is nothing there. It is just a city.

The shadow of the novel falls over you, weighty, material, as if capable of independent life. Make it stop. Make the making-up stop. The aim is not writing but life.[28]

As Hemingway said, no one's quite sure when an era begins, but everyone knows when it has ended. And the lovely way he said of Kiki,[29] she was never a lady, but she was the closest thing Montparnasse ever had to a queen.

The book closed. Never to be read for the first time again. Here's a space in time then.

The era began in the cold. And no, I didn't know it, didn't anticipate the weeks of summer that were to come. It was white and dry and cold. Firelight, a kind of compensatory sun.

Opened like a flower as the weather turned warmer. We went cycling in May when the lilac was in flower. The air was warm, and the lanes were full of lilac, and we picked great waving bunches of lilac. We got punch-drunk on lilac. So that when our panniers were full, we kept picking lilac anyway. We filled the house with lilac. We filled glasses and jars and bottles with lilac. The air in the house was close with the scent of lilac. There was no place in the house where lilac wasn't. We knew and understood lilac.[30]

That summer was full of light, clarity. Perhaps the last to be so completely full of light. How wonderful to write. Not to be alone. To be able to re-open the parcel, return. Limber, gangling summer. A heady artlessness. And so much light. "The sky above like a white bone."

That summer I grew taller. Only old men write like this. Summer was a daily occurrence. The daily miracle. The era was over before it began.

What is today?

Today is the first day of rain.[31]

Say goodbye to light and ease. It gets more difficult from here. The greater the summer the harder the fall. You lose your prince of light.

The sorry attempt to capture experience. Always that sad, little mournful attempt. Photographs that bear no resemblance to living, to experience. There's no warm air in a photograph. A bitter Parisian winter. Paucity. To have come this far for less not more. The era ends, the empire falls. Finish with a song. A canticle of heroism half heard, half guessed, half miracle, half hopelessness: *Nevertheless for his namesake, who can express the all that hangs to the wall? And sure that is grace. Remember me and be favoured as are everest and to thine people. Or is it veering our salvation that I* receive the felicity of thy chosen and the ice and madness. We are slipped with our fathers. We are daring and in debt in wickedly. Our fathers regarded the right timer in Egypt and live and kept able and regard the great goodness of inherit. That falling Ann and the did seeing that came in the Red Sea. Nevertheless he came forward and for his namesake. He who entered the Red Sea also and it was already dried up. He fought up on his mercies. And he gave. And he saved them from the other that we derived. He redoubted them and it was dried up so he led them through the deepest to the wildered. And he saved them from the adversaries. And delivered them from the hands of the enemy. As for those that tropical, these that tropical them, the waters were around them, there was not one of them left. And then he did in these parts and sang praises unto thee. Once within a while they forgot his glance. And would not his plights be answer. But lasting and pining in the great wilderness. And they tempted God in the desert. And he gave them every sign and said to be leave this where to. And said to be audience with to them song. The under take the sources and the takes. They undermined in grates. And ever *was thus the same for my ward. So they are same for my ward. So they aftered and wandered swaddled and wondered in dayful. And dark were the congregation of the mire. And for fire must they kingdom in their company. The flame went up in he and did reverie. They may not forfeit wine. And worshipped a bullseye gleamish. Blasted terminal in their glory into their similitude of a calf in threat he had made. Nevertheless when he saw their adversity, He marveled them on late. He fought upon his current and did walk onto and heeding them according unto the multitude of his mercies and he gave all of those that let him away the right to visit to return again.*

Supported initially by the brand descriptor, "the all over body spray".

The phone rings. Simon's voice: *I'm sorry I haven't called, I've been ill.* Your defence is your indifference. But now your indifference fails. You say, "I received your letter." You waited and waited and wished for that letter. You go on. "My friend Jenny died in hospital on 21st March 1997 – first day of spring.[32] I spent some of last Tuesday with her in hospital. She said she'd rather die quickly than slowly. And she died quickly. She was just 48 years old. I went to her funeral last week. At the wake, I noticed all of her shoes neatly arranged, ready to go somewhere, ready to step out."

Simon might come here this afternoon. You are stirred up by the idea of this afternoon's visit. In some ways you don't want to see Simon. You have retreated and Paris lives inside you, is peopled, great, austere, beautiful, inside you: everything that has occurred there – loves, bitter disappointments, triumph, new ideas, scandals, *succés fou*, mad love, the 20th Century, the future, the little magazines, the vernissages, the literary presses, the in-fighting, the alliances, intrigues, drawn battle lines, cafés, rain against the windows, a cold wind from the river, spring and summer barely hoped for, those annual miracles. A comfortable exchange of silence. There is the river, the bridge. There is the light, the wind, the island and its trees. There is Paris.

It seems there ought to be violence, sickness, horror, a high temperature to drive Simon out. The light holds us in the moment. In three weeks you have lived a lifetime, come close to despair, close to tears often, panic, violence and fury. You cannot be lovesick for a lily however lovely. And the eternal game: "Won't you miss me if we don't meet?" And the tight little knot of expectation, watching the clock, guarding time. The day hangs limply under cloud. And your hope is gone dark. And your optimism fails. And the time gnaws on. This is the curious thing about time. It is always in under or over supply.

You tell Simon, the cabaret singer you might engage said she normally charges £1000. But, you add, you don't know if she's any good. Simon replies: *If she's no good, just announce between songs that she usually costs £1000…*

The immense unfolding of life, its out-of-controlness. You find yourself run up the shore. You can describe your being here, but you can't reclaim the time, can't make the tide run again. When you are raw, unformed, you expect or want things to be smooth, superhuman, perfect. Then as you discover what's valuable you come to love the human in things, the ugly struggle for meaning. You come to appreciate flaws over flawlessness. You come to value raw insistence more than anything else. You appreciate the blind desire to go on. Effort is not smooth, knowing, efficient but wasteful, difficult, feckless, complacent, desperate, idle, half-hearted, vague, heartfelt, human.[33]

You can still conjure Simon all these years later after wars, economic crises, divorces:[34] the brown eyes fringed by dark spikes of lashes. It is easier to be unafraid when you confront things on your own terms. Once the ground is at a vertiginous tilt you are the better adapted. But if the terror and the recklessness are taken out of the picture, what's left? Was any of it substantial other than the way you used Simon as a punishment meted out to yourself? "Punishment for what?" you could ask. Punishment for not living at a stretch, spreading yourself one atom thin over the whole of possible experience.

We play *The Exquisite Corpse*:

Scones, especially those with currants in will envelop the hardest steel.

Tequila, but never Cinzano, to smooth the sharpest of edges.

Women don't like to be told by men that they are driving on the wrong side of the road.

Men need to be told that they are men.

Is it possible to realise who you are if no one really knows you, so no one can help?

No, I am not the first to be condemned because of who I'm not. I love no one.

Yes I am always responsible, it's because of who I am – people pretend they love me.

There are more things in this world than are dreamt of in your philosophies.

Do people love money or power more?

"Chile" is a funny name for such a hot country.

When you are not supposed to speak, the two of you speak easily, fluently. Suppose you were at lunch and supposed to speak, and were tongue-tied then, held back? "I envy you your voice," you'd say. "Mellifluous is the word, like ripe-fruit-flowing." Purple figs, melon. Fallen, over-ripe figs, and the fig tree with leaves like hands and the pavement underneath black-stained, treacherous with the flesh of the fallen fruit.

I had a dream of sounds, the first of my life. I saw all of the plate of continental Europe flat under the stars, the great mass of land, people, governments, war, between us. I so wanted to hear your voice. I longed to say, "I wanted to hear your voice." And to hear you say, *Here I am*. I woke up and it was as if you had spoken in the room.

I found this in a novel by Colette and it suits: "You're so unbearable and I'm so impossible."

The Cicadas make a silver, slippery sound on the hill above Taormina. The sun is long gone. The wind is up, threatening rain. The threat or the promise of something is in the air. Last night I asked myself what do I want? The cicadas ticked noisily. Stopped suddenly. And then nothing happened.

You are a wild brinkman, raw like a touch-sensitive plant, reckless, unthinking, once only. A miracle. And you called on Monday, on Tuesday, on Thursday, on Friday.

The two of you will have lunch on the South

Bank in a huge light-filled restaurant with the river outside and the clock at the top of the Shell Building dark against the sky. You watch the grey river outside, grey as your mood. The river is always astonishing. The enormous distance between its banks. The stone boxes of the big hotels with their backs to the river. The great hotels running like machines, showing their lights over the river at night, indicators of the life inside. The streaked stonework of the quays. White sky. And the lunch and the cold and the river make a brilliant blankness, not quite white, behind you. In that unforgiving light you'll appear paler than ever; your hands will tremble. You'll be thinner, hungrier. You were so hungry here once and there were only stale oranges in the kitchen.

Now you choose lunch: some soup, some fish, some white wine. You have little to say to one another. You've been asked here for the sake of writing, for the sake of art. You've been asked here so that you can upset life.

You have no idea how much Simon has seen or understood. You stay late into the afternoon.

You've sat for an extraordinary length of time. You've eaten very slowly, said very little. Sat in that terrible light, close to the window, unable to speak. That would be the end of you. The exhaustion would have become too great. The anxiety and the intensity of the desire to please would have become insupportable. You would be finished. The first part lost for ever and something less in its place with no power to drive you, a levelheadedness, a flat calm.

You can wish for life to be different in a hundred different ways, always to be driven by quiet dissatisfaction. You can want it to be shone up with a restlessness, a kind of uneven, mad life. But you do not consider what it might otherwise have been, how very hard in a practical way it might have been.

You can wear sorrow like a badge or it can be hidden so that it is not exterior to you at all but caught in the fibre. Then there is nothing redeeming or deepening about it. It's just sorrow, hard, numb sorrow.

The stones put there by the Greeks have seen

it all – another *Medea*,[35] another you. Lovers' names carved into the succulent paddles of cactus leaves, hundreds of bottles and tin cans discarded over a low wall. Young love, sex, procreation; decline, death. Death too, of imagination. An unbargained-for pregnancy, another discarded plastic bottle, another crowd of half-interested tourists "doing the Teatro Greco". And we were no different, brought back nothing different. "Broken stones in a hollow." And you didn't even get laid, behind the crumbling wall, where the dust turns in eddies, blown up from the sea.

Later it will rain in London yet again and the pavements will be smooth like the underside of fish. The café has no magic in it now; no liverish, unreal light because the bar heaters are switched off. You will not call. Will you have lunch together? If you imagine a thing a certain way, can it ever really turn out that way?

You are tongue-tied, embarrassed by one another. You are late or do not come. The food is bad. You see yourself sat in the terrible light from the windows; alone. You are not cruel, you are indifferent. But even indifference has a beautiful quality of tragedy about it. To be really damned is to be "quite liked".

They go to Paris and it is awful at first but then they see the city of light in its austere loveliness as if for the first time. Or they go to Paris and it is awful and they see nothing. They have nothing to bring to Paris, no hope, no imagination, only exhaustion and resignation. Paris is a failure because of them.

You altered things. You made the Seine gunmetal, beautiful; there was nothing of me in it. You made the café alive with *temperament*. There was nothing of me in any of it. I was incapable of reaction without you. I could act only under your tutelage.

A great dissatisfaction and you don't know why; an unrealistic expectation of what life might offer, perhaps. Or perhaps, worst of all, life is offering what it is unrealistic to expect and you just don't appreciate it. Do you defer to a future which may never come? You say, "I want to keep you clearly in my sights. I want you to help me. I want the greatest we are capable of. Conspire with me in this. If we are conspirators, nothing else can cloud or confuse. The battle is won before it's fought." Rain in hot places always strikes me as a miracle or a gift, altering the light momentarily in some important way. The rain-filled pool overflows continuously; the waiters worry about the furniture; the cloud has burst its flank. The sea turns pale as the rain falls across it. You are a discovery or even an invention; something necessary.

Lunch on the South Bank by the river. You are gently mocking. "Well, here's luck!"[36] And how profound is the effect of a glass of red wine; the second glass even more so. If you do not drink, you shrink from the enemy but a vodka martini from the bar – transparent, pure, concentrate – has the effect of a half-bottle of wine in one small violently cold glass. You were changed so suddenly, so instantaneously that the change had already occurred before you were aware of it. You discovered this kinship with alcohol a long time ago but still it catches you by surprise every time.

You are pleased.

So little is the substance of the artist's life; you are so easily pleased.

You do have lunch. On a blank, cold, windy day with nothing otherwise to commend it. "I'll wait for you and if you don't come, I'll eat alone. I think that you won't come. And that will put a glorious end to that. As I wait for you, I'll write, I'll get it all down. I want to sit against the light. I want to be drenched, bleached, made anaemic. You will see everything, the fear, the shadows under my eyes, the strange ridges that appear just above the cheek bones when I haven't slept; strange swellings, collections of lymphatic fluid."

Fear. Not the fear that violent feeling will become violent action but fear with no object like damp in the fabric of a house. Simple. Unmeetable. Fear describes its own horizon. You have not yet come to terms with the idea that writing is entirely arbitrary, that it is as frail as you are. This is what making art is, a frailty.[37] This is the truth of it.

They do meet for lunch in the restaurant like

a glasshouse with the river beyond. They do meet. And the day is blank. And you do not understand what is at stake. They meet and the talk comes easily. You are light, elastic, easy. You have anticipated, invented this moment. They have come to a fictional lunch. You said, "We'll have a long lunch, hours long, and some good red wine. And at the very end, when it's all hopeless over cigars, we'll see what we will see."

They do go to lunch. They've sat at one of the sheet glass windows.

You have already drunk a great deal of wine when Simon arrives. You talk about Shakespeare, Gertrude Stein. You eat. You are held back. You remember nothing. You are waiting for the right moment for it to be finished. Then you say you'll probably never see each other again; you'll make certain of it. It's this and nothing more. This is all of it. Later it is all nothing. And neither of you understands what is really going on.

Then I'll say you have shored me up; it's extraordinary the effect you have on me. And in the telling of all of this is the beginning of our end.

With the blank light from the windows and the river nothing more than an obscure, slow-moving shadow beyond your shoulder. I have drunk too much. I hold nothing back, I'm in your hands, to finish us, to murder us off.

You sit very quietly. And then you reply *I've known for some time.* You smile and the deep etches appear at the corners of your mouth. Your eyes are spires. Whyever write that? The waiters want us to leave. The restaurant is empty. You pay the bill. We are leaving because you have understood nothing. We have lunch. They do have lunch in the restaurant with its glass-walled dining room. You say, you had no idea. You cannot be important to anyone.

They did meet. The light was nothing more than a blankness. The lunch was an end.

Do you measure yourself against other people's understanding of you or do you expect them to understand you in a certain way and so they do? One star in the sky. The North Star you suppose. (The waiter murmured there was going to be a storm. We waited. Smoked another cigar. We sat and looked at the waiter and the waiter looked right back, rolled his shoulders. Smiled.)

It becomes difficult to see the room around you, the page, as if you were turned in on yourself. Your own work is a great consolation for something. You just don't know why you need consoling. You bristle in the world. Only a thought or reasoned insistence makes it through to you.

(In the back streets away from the cafés and clothes shops, a cobbler mending shoes in a dark little room that gave straight onto the street – hammering the sole of a shoe upturned on the last like a figure from ancient history; something from the Greek Tragedy.)

I tell you I have been writing here. I don't explain everything. I don't explain that I've written out our futures for us. I tell you I can't say too much or there will be no point in meeting. I say I'll show you everything afterwards. I'll sit in front of you in the blank light from the river and tell you everything. I look directly ahead. I fix you in my sights and give up whatever sovereignty over myself I have left. I'll be brittle as a leaf skeleton. There'll be nothing left of me, only this trembling and the desire to be near you as the sudden source of so much unanticipated life.

You say, *In case you were wondering* – and I don't know what I'm supposed to have been wondering about. You say you have to grow a beard for the part you're going play. You laugh and say you can't grow a convincing beard and the spare, dark lines of the beard spring from flesh as soft and as a white as the flesh of a girl's throat. There is something affecting about the thin fibres, neatly ordered against skin all but untouched by time.[38]

You do go to lunch. They do have lunch. And you tell it plainly, "I thought each of us was master of his own destiny. And then we met. And I traded everything for the desire to write one small story, almost without incident, about you."

What is it we really want? To live an emblematic life. The emblems are so much more compelling than the life that stands behind them – *The Fictional City of Paris*,[39] not Paris; *The Legendary Artist*, not the living; *The Unknown You*, not the known; *The Emblematic Writer's Life*, not the grinding, daily life of the writer; not a well-balanced, well-proportioned life but one burnished up, inflamed, maddened.

It was as if there was no light in you. You were just there. We were ordinary. How are we to "earn death" if all of life is levelled in this way?

And then, this afternoon, you stayed longer than you needed to. You said, *My mother is puritanical about everything but sex*. And we are saved. Now something much more dangerous occurs. I see you. Not the idea of you. But you yourself. "Here's Luck!"

The idea of anticipating lunch together, writing possible scenarios longhand in a mid-blue notebook. Living into what I have written; life from writing rather than writing from life.

The impossibility of the complete capture of life by anything other than life.

Katya was playing *Suite Bergamasque* last night; and I saw us all, carrying on our lives, having our moment in the light before we're swept away, replaced by time.

When you rode in a cable car for the first time, you hadn't anticipated the elasticity in the cable; it was like floating on water.

The invitation to Simon reads: *Lunch. Upstairs at the Festival Hall. Table booked for 12.45 in the name of "Lol Stein"*.[40] In a film script the mise-en-scène would read: *they eat lunch by one of the tall windows with its plate glass greenish like the sea and the dark wash of the river beyond.* What an ambition to be wholly available to another person (wearing every one of your failings with pride). You are both oddly appalled that you have met like this. Is it necessary to speak even? You sit in silence. Nothing is hidden. "If you come I know you will be wholehearted. And if you prefer not to come I will understand." The aim is to ask too much, of course. We should aim for, and demand, and expect too much of each other as a matter of principle. You are raw, direct, clear. You are intent on living to the brink of ruin or it's not living at all. In the appalling light from the greenish glass, with the river dragging by beyond, something will take place. You'll dare. You'll be afraid and you'll "forgive me a little fear". We'll make something of ourselves. The business of Tuesday 17th, lunch. The restaurant will run on around us, a sort of imperious, glazed business taking place all around us and we'll be lost in courage and mutual demand. Which version of lunch eventually occurs? Which of the written versions will you gift to reality? Now you have read the first few lines carefully, you say you are afraid of what might happen, of what might be said. You say, "Do we really have anything to lose? And do we really have any choice now?" You have both come knowingly. The first glasses are for courage only, metallic, sickly. You sit with your back to the light. This is very important. It is important to you that you are appallingly well lit; and if the threads of blood are visible, pulling under the skin of your face, so much the better.

I have written out our lives for us. Before it occurred to me that we might meet unflinchingly, I wrote a pale, gentle future for us. I wrote the beginning of the story, what amounts to an invitation, and the future became less certain. The pale version of the future is already written. I could predict an acceptable future for us very simply. But what might the new story, the new future be? We might astonish/appall/ruin ourselves. Write a future. Record what it would be impossible to invent. You are free to follow a whim, free to weight the moment. The only possible failure is to turn yourself over to forces less than yourself.

You were so afraid, you nearly cancelled lunch. You don't know what you were afraid of, life perhaps. Perhaps the reckless, ruinous entanglement you've been writing about so gleefully. You were afraid but you also understood that if you shy away from life, everything is lost. Everything you profess to believe in would turn out to be a theoretical certainty only. Life itself would be lost. In other words, there is the risk you are a coward.

Once that's understood, things don't seem so bad and you can embrace "a sort of standing without defence". Our flaws worn openly might make us worth knowing. You are the architect with full responsibility for the life to be built; not the life imagined or wished for, but built. It has a wide, distant, tangible horizon, this life. It requires a correspondent, someone like Simon who'll take seriously the experiment to write into life. Of course you are still afraid. Fear – being bound by it or released from it – lies in the minutest details. You feel the world magnified one hundredfold over. And had you cancelled lunch or were Simon not to turn up, you would have negated yourself in some way, negated all of your attempts at writing, at living.

You have faith that there can be no such thing as an unpleasant truth. See me in the unforgiving light after a night of disturbed sleep. See my hair thinning. See I am afraid. See I drink for support. See I am as afraid as you.

How do you format, intentionally, the live performance of life as the actual moments unfold? You do not allow yourselves to speak. This is the first step. You are silent. You look at each other.

You cap yourselves like an oil well until the pressure of the desire to speak becomes intolerable. I tell you something true. I say I am pleased we are here, that it's Tuesday 17th, that there is no sun today. I have already written about the quality of the light, blank light at the windows, a goose-weather sky. I say I cannot imagine writing into life in this way with anyone else. I have had to direct myself outwardly, extend myself out into the world to reach you. I do not know what you will reply. I cannot write that far into life.

It is essential for the purposes of the experiment to say too much, drink too much, rush headlong toward what may, or may not, be ruin. You cry because of the alcohol. A terrible mawkish romanticism has entered the proceedings. You cry simply because you are capable of it. You are wholly available to yourself. Frayed, over-emotional, tired, drunk, absolutely committed without caveats or concessions. And you'll never have lived through anything like it before. You wished for this moment with its terrible, rising panic; all the colour bleached out of life.

You stood in the garden awkwardly, like a fool, sickening yourself because all you wanted was to stand nearby. Why do you burn? Why is your body so full of heat? You are sickened by the remnants of alcohol. So much work and so much life. The difficulty now is the distortion you'll inevitably bring to your recollection of this time together. You'll make things up. Everything will seem significant by virtue of your having said or thought it. Write literature not a lovelorn diary. Sweat the work out of yourself.

You were ahead. On the bridge. You were crossing over at the same time. The river water peeling away in thick brown coils and the wind raising waves on the river. You held back, a little, deliberately. Waited in the wind-shadow of the embankment wall. You could have caught up but you were afraid of meeting too soon. You were easy to recognise, even from that distance, because of the distinctive way you move. You're recognisable at a thousand paces because of the way you carry yourself. You arrive and you are very warm. You are slightly out of control, pan-icked (Pan, half man, half goat, god of all things wild, and of alcohol). You have to sit somewhere quietly, alone. You have to try to regulate your own behaviour. You have to attempt to appear sane.

The waiter says, "Your guest is already here." And there you are, without your glasses, clear in the light from the windows, just as it had been written days, weeks earlier. Your fringe falls in small tails against your forehead because you are warm too. You have a beer.

I ask for a vodka martini. I say, "These work instantly."[41] I am nervous, afraid. I have books for you: P.D. Ouspensky and Marguerite Duras. I hand them over because it is something to do, something to ameliorate the terrible fact of our being together.

You ask about the significance of "Lol Stein".

I reply, "It is in the Duras – *The Ravishing of Lol V. Stein*." The horrendous, remorseless truth of Duras.[42]

You tell me you are waiting for something to be revealed.

I tell you I have written all this already. I have written into life and you must read it. But I say the revelation, if there is to be one, must come from you. I can't do it all by myself. This delights you. You talk about Jean Rhys.[43] You drink some wine called *Stoney Vale*. You eat.

I say the light is just right. I look at you and you are not a real thing to me. You are full of light. Blank. Terrible. There is the finest line at the corner of your mouth. I watch this line, love you for it.

The alcohol and the panic consume your memory. O yes, Pan is here. There are holes in the afternoon. You know these are the well-fed moments so smooth they've not grazed the surface memory.

And then I tell you. In the terrible light from the windows. I tell you, as I always intended, I tell you I believe our destinies have been forged together.

You take up the idea, say you believe in linked destinies independent of sexuality or gender.

I see us very clearly at the edge. I remind you of my last letter, of my longing to be approved of by you and you tell me, *About that, O I do.* I talk about Paris. I say it is more beautiful than is imaginable. I talk about *The Atlas Press* and *Oulipo.*[44] A soft death waits for you. The dinosaur surviving the crunch. There is only one way for you to survive, the hardest thing, flattest, plainest truth. Have you described your position adequately enough? Have you said enough unequivocally? Just you. Wrong or right. The old familiar self-disregard. Your imagination makes the most elaborate constructions: "You're embarrassing us! How do you exist in the real world. How do you have the audacity to go on?"

You decide to go to Paris. You pay your bill, take a cab to fetch your passports and you'll be in Paris by the early evening. Will you? Is it possible?

I say we must share a room, just for me to be in a room with another living thing. Paris is a kind of death. We must share so there will be another living thing in the room – against the effrontery of death. And you agree. Simply. You nod. Just like that. You are from another world.

Cigars. You say we must have the biggest. A kind of madness descends. Another bottle of *Stoney Vale*. The fire of the lit cigar. Limpid holes burn open in memory. And you will be another living thing for me in the room in Paris in the night. A kind of death, Paris.

The waiter asks you to leave because it is so late. Last of the sun above the plane trees. Sand banked up against the quay wall because the tide is low. (If you have grown up near the sea you are always aware of your distance from it.) I suggest the bar of the Waldorf Hotel because it has the loveliest gilt chairs – plump plush backs and beautifully turned feet – answering even the possibility of defeat with an unthinkingly heroic frivolity.

You do not remember the bridge across the Thames. You remember feeling Simon's disappointment about Paris. You knew you wouldn't go. Simon knew it too. Later Simon admits he was banking on your not going. Just as you were banking on Simon's willingness to go!

Paris would have been two different things to us. An amusement for Simon. A variety of death for you.

Everything has turned the colour of an ear or a shell, a toe, the tip of a tongue, Turkish delight, Arabian roses, shells, pomegranates, rose quartz.

Outside Charing Cross at rush hour, taxis pull in, stop, pull out. A taxi home? To Heathrow? You are crushed by the idea that you have disappointed. You want to be regarded as extraordinary, courageous, great; not fearful, incapable of adventure. And Charing Cross and rush hour and the crowds of people are suddenly lost, displaced. The sound fades.

I am looking at you and there is only you under the sweltering sky. You are smiling at me benignly with no idea of what I'm saying. I'm saying I will go to Paris if you will understand what it means. And then I am saying nothing. I said Paris was nothing. I have no idea how long I stand there, saying Paris is nothing, how long we stand outside Charing Cross, how long the taxis and buses pass inaudibly. There is no world. You are the world. You represent all those things I have claimed to believe in: open-mindedness, making ourselves into something worthwhile by our own efforts. Every reference by which I have navigated living is now gone, swept away, and the world is replaced by you.

There is the light from the sky and there is you.

YOURS ALWAYS
and UNBEATEN

The sea appears on the right suddenly, washing the edge of the plain. Twin lagoons and the town built between the two, a fort on the hill, the headland, the farthest point, like a limb flung out. The sky is black. Of course it's not cold but wet and terrible. Shutters banging. A car alarm some way off. The sky blazes in one direction only. The sea is full of light, rippled. Strange that it is far more beautiful now.

O and now the most extraordinary gun-crack of thunder high up inside the cloud. Bird song. What are the birds so pleased about? Now the thunder merges into one sustained, implacable growl. Rain in earnest. A yacht rolls in the harbour. (They'll be throwing up in the staterooms.) The bay is patterned over with weird islands of light and dark, as if the water were different depths or temperatures. All that's needed now is a plague of locusts. "I am always impatient for more," I used to say. There is no displacement between the lightning and the thunder. The building shakes. The windows may shatter. Now part of the building has been struck. People running. Darkness. Biblical proportions to this storm. The rain is so hard it's stripping the leaves from the trees. Gargoyles, chins jutting into the cloisters, explain themselves suddenly by spewing cataracts of dirty water. *Absinthe makes the heart grow fonder.* It's like deep sea diving or space walking. The storm has drawn mud down the mountainside and out into the sea, great plumes of it fanning open, turning the sea seal-coloured, uncannily pale. The wooden saint on the landing appears to be someone waiting for me, immobile but not inanimate. And then the lightning comes and I see it is just wood and gilt. I think about guilt sometimes. The physicality of the landscape, the heat, wet, mountains – everything makes sense of the strength of religion – bastion monasteries, stone madonnas, mountaintop crucifixes, superstition, terror in the night, Catholicism, incense, salvation. And, too, the urgency for physical contact; children, dynasty, continuation. I ask myself, am I prepared to answer for my actions? And, so far, the answer has always been, yes.

The pen is mightier than the sordid. I miss speaking to you, especially when you would appear unannounced and we would share a bottle of wine. It was like finding a pearl on the beach – more than one could reasonably hope for. *Courage in the face of perversity.* From the square at Taormina, the sicilian youth very dark, Greek-looking, with hair sculpted into curious ridges and devil's horns, drinking Vecchia Romagna and espresso.

Today, in a small antiquarian bookshop, I found the autobiography of St. Teresa of Ávila.[45] I opened a page at random and there the life of a saint was described as *silence and inactivity.* I wrote somewhere that we should long for time to become vast, meaningless and then, in the meaninglessness of time, astonishing amounts of work could be done. It has something to do with imagination – elasticity even – forgiveness.

The aria *All My Long Life* at the end of the

Thompson/Stein opera *The Mother of Us All*;[46] this need for life span, the space and stretch of an entire life. The road to lucidity is very long, very hard and the yield sparse along the way. You tried to make something perfectly fluid, lyric, because you thought then it might be so closely structured it would catch it all (like a very fine net).

Everything depends on the quality of our encounter with the world at lunch (I've just written "at lunch" instead of "at large"). An idea can be corralled, mapped by language, even if it cannot be described by it. Perhaps all our efforts are concerned with plotting the edges (and so the whereabouts, the structure) of the unwordable.

Did I tell you about the first Roman Catholic Evensong I ever heard? I understood more, though the Latin was meaningless to me, than I had ever understood from an Anglican mass. The frame or phenomenon that contains all action and potential-to-act but is never active itself. A boundary. The discovery of the interval. The disparity between meaning and understanding. I enjoy the idea of being pressed to something for a very long time (all my long life). Old assumptions cannot survive the coming of a new ideas. You cannot go back. The flag moves behind the eyes, you feel it. I can hear the piano, faintly from inside the house; a tractor somewhere. The life of a saint is not so different from our own. Change the semantics and it's all there – struggle, false hope, vanity; relinquishment on a vast scale; faith, vision.

You aim for an experience which is superfluous, nothing to do with utility, but which gives the higher faculties (whatever that may mean) joy. Saint Teresa of Ávila: "It is a glorious bewilderment, a heavenly madness, in which true wisdom is acquired." We can agree about madness at least; wisdom is something other than sanity, other than the world's idea of what it is to be sane. Later Saint Teresa talks about the difficulty of explaining prayer: "I have never understood it or been able to explain it. I decided therefore that when I came to this place in my narrative I would say little or nothing about it."

The presence of another soul for the first

time. You see the soul perhaps. It's frightening (or frightening not to if we are only what we can make of ourselves, as Ouspensky believed). The possibility of failing in the attempt is to be properly alive. At least, let us be properly alive.

Everything is swept away suddenly – all of the old assumptions collapse. We are changed into something else. It is the happiness of being irreplaceable in another's existence.

An unheard voice may as well not have spoken: the thought may as well have occurred and remained shuttered up by the skull-bones of the thinker.

I don't leave you behind. I don't leave anyone behind. I carry it all with me. Whole worlds inside me. You arrived here, scrubbed, hurried, saying *I forgot what time we said, I finished work late and so I hurried, showered, here I am. What time did we say?*

Secretly observed intimacies – a mole, a birth mark. I asked you if I could touch your hand.

You thanked me for the wine, said it was just what you had needed. I think of you now by the garden gate thanking me. Years have passed. Years of anxiety, denial, satiation, collapse, rally, abandonment, work. We've become nothing to one another. But I still hold and care for the memory of you.

It is late. I go into the over-lit great hall alone. The light blares down from huge, cage-like chandeliers. The pianist is playing an old dilapidated grand poorly. I order a glass of champagne. I've taken a book with me – that great standby of The Alone and The Lonely. I read. The champagne is very cold. Bitter. I drink half the glass. I'm alone. Independent even of the prop, my book. I am a fact. A physical, happily stated fact, contained and contented in myself.

And then I find myself gazing at the open door. I smile at this calamitous failing. My easy capitulation – that's the word, capitulation. After everything. After the heat in difficult places,[47] the pain, the dissatisfaction, the gain, loss and collapse, the running of time, confusions and contradictions, after all of this, after everything said and not said, mostly not said, after all this I would have you walk through the open door. I would take you on any terms, any way to exist in relation to you. I am nothing but my feeling for you. There is no detail, no special truth, no substance or calculation in it. My feeling is empty, only space; vast, emptying substancelessness. I am absent but for my feeling for you. Nothing can describe the great sweep of my feeling for you. I am nothing but my feeling for you.

Saint Teresa (of prayer): "There is no power left in the body – and the soul possesses none – by which the joy can be communicated…. sometimes I find it a help to utter nonsense."

Perhaps the idea of "uttering nonsense" – and the thought that you might hear me – makes it possible for me to speak with conviction. The idea that you might really be listening (at your most thoughtful, most fully pressed to the task of understanding) makes it not only possible but necessary for me to speak.

FIN

NOTES

(1)

Gertrude Stein and her brother Leo moved to London in the autumn of 1902. Leo left for Paris in December, Gertrude remained at 20 Bloomsbury Square until February 1903. She found London depressing because of the "dead weight of that fog".

(2)

In the early 19th Century, the Elgin Marbles were removed from the Acropolis in Athens by agents of Thomas Bruce, 7th Earl of Elgin. They are displayed in the Duveen Gallery of the British Museum in London, a dedicated exhibition space opened in 1939, funded by the art dealer Sir Joseph Duveen. A long-standing dispute continues over the ownership of the Elgin Marbles. The Greek government disputes the legality of their removal and seeks their return to the Parthenon.

(3)

A tool called a pointing iron is used to introduce, shape and smooth mortar between cobble stones.

(4)

In 1956, Charles Ritz, chairman of the Ritz in Paris, asked if Hemingway was aware that a trunk of his was in a basement storage room, left there in 1930.

Hemingway did not remember storing the trunk but did recall Louis Vuitton had made a special trunk for him in the 1920s. Hemingway had wondered what happened to it. Charles Ritz had the trunk brought up to his office, and after lunch Hemingway opened it. It was filled with a ragtag collection of clothes, menus, receipts, memos, hunting and fishing paraphernalia, skiing equipment, racing forms, correspondence and, on the bottom, something that elicited a joyful reaction from Hemingway: "The notebooks! So that's where they were! Enfin!" There were two stacks of lined notebooks like the ones used by schoolchildren in Paris when he lived there in the '20s. Hemingway had filled them with his careful handwriting while sitting in his favourite café, nursing a café crème. The notebooks described the places, the people, the events of his penurious life in Paris, and formed the basis of *A Moveable Feast*.

(5)

Prior to Moroccan independence in 1956, Tangier was an International Zone administered by a coalition of nations. The city became an important gathering place for bohemians and intellectuals, many of whom were homosexual or bisexual, creating a vibrant and open atmosphere. Paul Bowles and his wife Jane were both bisexual and their bohemian lifestyle in Tangier included a vibrant peer group of gay artists and writers.

(6)

The chapter *Sentences and Paragraphs* in *How to Write* by Gertrude Stein (1931) begins, "A sentence is not emotional a paragraph is". The text continues with observations like, "A sentence has colors when they mean I liked it as selling salt should be very little used in dishes." And, "Think of a use for a paragraph. A sentence is exhausted by have they been there with him. A useful and useful if you add house you have a paragraph."

(7)

C. Farr's dissatisfaction with language is apparent in this seminal passage. The description of a thing is not the thing itself. It does not live because it is described. Other strategies are necessary. These observations echo Cubist theory, ascribed to Picasso by Gertrude Stein but invented by her according to the journalist Janet Flanner. Stein maintained that cubists painted not what they could see but what they knew to be there because they had evidences other than the evidence of their senses.

(8)

The more usual expression would be "glowing heart". Farr's "growing heart" is a deliberate choice, intended to evoke the accelerating emotional development of the protagonist.

(9)

If champagne is served too cold, there are fewer bubbles, the taste buds are numbed, and the aromas are less pronounced. Served too warm, and the carbon dioxide in the champagne will be released too quickly and too profusely, disrupting the flavour and reducing the quality of the tasting. To make the most of champagne's complexity, it should be served at between 46°F and 50°F (8°C – 10°C). The ideal serving temperature will also vary depending on the age and type of champagne. The oldest bottles, rosés, vintage champagnes, and grand cuvées should be served between 53.5°F and 57°F (12°C – 14°C) in order to reveal their greater complexity.

(10)

cf. Hemingway's comments on living in Paris from the opening of *A Moveable Feast* (1964): "If you are lucky enough to have lived in Paris as a young man, then wherever you go for the rest of your life, it stays with you, for Paris is a moveable feast."

(11)

In her cook book, Alice B. Toklas wrote that black coffee made her feel "lively and courageous".

(12)

A reference to the Tao, in which the aim is to live in harmonious accord with the fundamental nature of the universe, rather than to struggle against it. Living in this way, one realises that everything needed is already close to hand.

(13)

In collaboration with the poet, Edith Sitwell, William Walton (29 March 1902 – 8 March 1983) had his first great success as a composer in 1923. *Façade* was performed in public at the Aeolian Hall, London, on 12 June. The work consisted of Edith's verse, which she recited through a megaphone from behind a curtain by English painter Frank Dobson, while Walton conducted an ensemble of six, playing his accompanying music. *Façade* was a *succès de scandale*. *The Daily Express* deplored the work, but admitted that it was naggingly memorable. *The Manchester Guardian* described it as "relentless cacophony". *The Observer* condemned the verses and dismissed Walton's music as "harmless". *Façade* is now, of course, regarded as one of the most important modernist works of the 20th Century.

(14)

Leon-Bollée is another reference to the work of Marguerite Duras. She revisited the events of her novel *The Lover* in a new work called *The North China Lover* (1991). As the title suggests, the new text provides greater detail about her love affair with a much older Chinese man in French Indochina: "I describe how I took his hand and put it on my genitals when he picked me up for the first time in his big black car, a legendary Morris-Léon Bollée."

(15)
Goose Weather is the title of the first chapter of Edith Sitwell's book *The English Eccentrics* (1933): "In this strange 'goose-weather', when even the snow and the black-fringed clouds seem like old theatrical properties, dead players' cast-off rags, 'the complexion of a murderer in a bandbox, consisting of a large piece of burnt cork, and a coal-black Peruke', and when the wind is so cold that it seems like an empty theatre's 'Sea, consisting of a dozen large waves, the tenth a little bigger than ordinary, and a little damaged', I thought of those medicines that were advised for Melancholy, in the Anatomy of this disease, of mummies made medicine, and of the profits of Dust-sifting."

(16)
The thing that is "not nice" is Christianity's wholesale assimilation – or Christianisation – of indigenous pagan tradition in the British Isles.

(17)
You see it long before you reach it, that great tower rising out of the barley fields somewhere near the middle of Norfolk. The church of St Peter and St

Paul stands almost alone with only a couple of Victorian buildings and a cricket pitch for company. Salle church, an exceptionally complete Perpendicular building, dates from the first part of the 15th century. The tower, 111 ft (34 m) tall, faced with Barnack stone and flint, was built during the period 1422-1461 with the exception of the top storey which was added at the end of the 15th Century. It has been described as "the most perfectly composed of all late medieval Norfolk towers" and as "one of the first of the great East Anglian towers".

(18)
Erik Satie (17 May 1866 – 1 July 1925), French composer and pianist. His works for solo piano, three *Gymnopédies* (1888) and six *Gnossiennes* (1893/1968), are characterised by simplicity, repetition, and highly original modal harmonies. Satie's description of his approach to composition might equally be applied to the present volume: "To have a feeling for harmony is to have a feeling for tonality... the melody is the Idea, the outline; as much as it is the form and the subject matter of a work. The harmony is an illumination, an exhibition of the object, its reflection."

(19)
The editor of the present volume made a number of small requests, one of which was for more detail

about the person known only as "Louise" in the original manuscript. In response, Farr added the editor's request to the text for publication along with the response that they were unable to comply because they had no further recollection of Louise.

(20)
Alice B. Toklas, "Gypsy Goulash": 1½ lb. fillet of beef in slices of ¼ inch thickness, cut in lengths of ¼ inch width, browned in lard with 1 teaspoon salt, 1 tablespoon paprika, and 1 tablespoon flour, 4 large onions sliced, ¾ lb. potatoes sliced. When lightly browned add 2 cups of red wine, 1 cup sour cream, and enough *bouillon* to cover. Put in covered casserole in 375° oven for 1 hour. Add ½ cup sour cream before serving. Serve with noodles. Serves 4.

(21)
cf. Gertrude Stein's "continuous present". Stein wrote *Composition as Explanation* in the winter of 1925–26 and delivered it as a lecture to the Cambridge Literary Club and at Oxford University that summer. It was published later the same year by Leonard and Virginia Woolf's Hogarth Press. Stein discusses her embrace of the "prolonged present" and "continuous present" rather than the traditional past, present, and future tenses: "So then I as a contemporary creating the composition in the beginning was groping toward a continuous present,

a using everything a beginning again and again and then everything being alike then everything very simply everything was naturally simply different and so I as a contemporary was creating everything being alike was creating everything naturally being naturally simply different, everything being alike."

(22)

The twelve-tone technique is most often attributed to Austrian composer Arnold Schoenberg (13 September 1874 – 13 July 1951). Instead of using one or two tones as main points of focus for an entire composition (as key centres in tonal music), Schoenberg suggested using all twelve tones "related only to one another". In Schoenberg's system, no notes would predominate as focal points, nor would any hierarchy of importance be assigned to the individual tones. The new unifying principle in composition would then arise from the particular order given to a collection of the twelve tones, an order that would be different for each composition. By referring to twelve-tone technique and the idea of "better tools for the job", Farr likens their own attempts at compositional innovation to Schoenberg's.

(23)

Tosca is a three-act Italian opera by Giacomo Puccini with a libretto by Luigi Illica and Giuseppe Giacosa.

First performed at the Teatro dell'Opera di Roma in January 1900, a contemporary critic described it as a "tawdry little shocker". The mise-en-scène is Rome, 1800, at a time of political upheaval and revolution. The action concerns a love triangle between the opera singer Floria Tosca, her lover, a freedom fighter called Mario Cavaradossi, and the corrupt Chief of Police, Baron Scarpia. Scarpia lusts after Tosca and misuses his power and position in an attempt to possess her. During a religious service in the church of Sant'Andrea della Valle, prompted by lust, he sings, "Tosca, you make me forget God!"

(24)
The strongest form of expression is the one closest to the source with least possible deviation from it. Gertrude Stein used to say that the writer must learn to hear their inner voice. The reason writers have to revise their texts is because they have not learned to hear the inner voice accurately enough. When the communication is clear and direct, the text is true first time and no revision is necessary.

(25)
The nature of individual elements is less important than the relationship between them. What is of primary importance in life, as in art, is the way different episodes/elements occur or are placed in relation to one another.

(26)

"Bubbles rising in a pan of water" echoes a line from Virginia Woolf's novel, *The Waves* (1931): "Bubbles form on the floor of the saucepan," said Jinny. "Then they rise, quicker and quicker, in a silver chain to the top." Woolf's novel, arguably her most experimental in form, is composed of the interior monologues of its six characters: Bernard, Susan, Rhoda, Neville, Jinny and Louis. The textural reference "bubbles rising" allies C. Farr's attempt to find new form with *The Waves'* experimentalism.

(27)

Self-Portrait with Raphaelesque Neck. Salvador Dali. c. 1921. Oil on canvas. 40.5 x 53cm. Unsigned and undated. Fundació Gala-Salvador Dalí, Figueres, Spain.

(28)

Farr aims to avoid conventional narrative style but admits that the precedent of "the novel" makes it difficult to strike out over new ground free of historical or cultural influence.

(29)

Alice Ernestine Prin (2 October 1901 – 29 April 1953), nicknamed the Queen of Montparnasse and often known as Kiki de Montparnasse, was a French model, chanteuse, memoirist and painter during the

Jazz Age. She flourished in, and helped define, the liberated culture of Paris in the *Années folles* of the 1920s. She became one of the most famous models of the 20th century and in the history of avant-garde art. In 1929, she published an autobiography, *Kiki's Memoirs*, with introductions by Ernest Hemingway and Tsuguharu Foujita. The book was reprinted illicitly throughout the 1950s and 1960s under the title, *The Education of a Young Model.* Long after her death, Prin remains the embodiment of the outspokenness, audacity and creativity that marked the interwar period in Montparnasse.

(30)
cf. Lines 1 - 4 *The Waste Land* by T.S. Eliot:
April is the cruellest month, breeding
Lilacs out of the dead land, mixing
Memory and desire, stirring
Dull roots with spring rain.

(31)
cf. Jacques Prévert:
Chanson
Quel jour sommes-nous
Nous sommes tous les jours
Mon amie
Nous sommes toute la vie
Mon amour
Nous nous aimons et nous vivons

Nous vivons et nous nous aimons
Et nous ne savons pas ce que c'est que la vie
Et nous ne savons pas ce que c'est que le jour
Et nous ne savons pas ce que c'est que l'amour.

Song
What day are we?
We are every day
My friend
We're all life
My love
We love and we live
We live and we love
And we don't know
What life is
And we don't know
What the day is
And we don't know
What love is

Prévert's poetry, especially his collection *Paroles*, has been described as "paper tablecloth" poetry. *Paroles* was compiled from various sources, including newspaper clippings, cabaret songs, and notes jotted down on paper tablecloths in cafes; hence the name. The method of composition ties Prévert's poetry to everyday experiences and settings, mirroring the life he observed and wrote about.

(32)

Comet Hale-Bopp was visible for about 18 months from May 1996 to December 1997. This seemed significant to her friends; a light in the sky for Jenny Cole.

(33)

The ugly, failed and struggled for may also be the truest form of all.

(34)

cf. French novelist Marguerite Duras in *The Lover* (1984): "Years after the war, after marriages, children, divorces, books, he came to Paris with his wife."

(35)

Medea is a tragedy by Euripides, first performed in Athens in 431 BC. It tells the story of Medea who, betrayed by her husband Jason, exacts a terrible revenge – she murders both Jason's new wife and her own two sons. In the closing action, Euripides presents Medea as he presented many indisputably divine beings in other plays. Just like these other gods, Medea interrupts and halts the violent actions of mortals on the lower plane. She justifies her terrible revenge on the grounds that she has been treated with disrespect and mockery.

(36)

cf. *After Leaving Mr Mackenzie* (1931) by Jean Rhys:
"She shook her head and began to sip mechanically.
'Well, here's luck!' said Mr Horsfield, sighing.
'Chin-Chin!' said Julia. Over the rim of her glass her
eyes looked cloudy and dazed."

(37)

Authority over what is good or bad is not external
to the maker. All art is frail. Maker and thing-made
are unquantifiable to all at first sighting. Nothing is
right or wrong, good or bad except by virtue of its
inner cohesion.

(38)

In the Athens of ancient Greece, same-sex
relationships were formalised by tradition: an older
man would act as *erastes* to a young boy, his *eromeno*.
When the boy started to develop facial hair, he
would be cast aside because the relationship was
supposed to be a temporary one, part of the
education of the young. The boy was expected to
become an *erastes* in his own turn and, eventually, to
marry a woman.

(39)

cf. The fictional city of Mahagonny in Kurt Weil's
opera, *Aufstieg und Fall der Stadt Mahagonny / Rise and
Fall of the City of Mahagonny*. The protagonist of

November 17th is "writing up" the lovers' destinies, including their triumph or defeat in a similarly fictional version of Paris. The question becomes which of these fictional possibilities will solidify as lived reality.

(40)
cf *Le ravissement de Lol V. Stein/The Ravishing of Lol Stein* (1964) by Marguerite Duras: "That she had so completely recovered her sanity was a source of sadness to her. One should never be cured of one's passion."

(41)
cf. Sally Bowles in *Goodbye to Berlin* (1939) by Christopher Isherwood: *"Would you like a prairie oyster?" She produced glasses, eggs and a bottle of Worcestershire from the boot-cupboard under the dismantled washstand. "I practically live on them." Dexterously she broke the eggs into the glasses, added the sauce and stirred the mixture with the end of a fountain pen. "They're about all I can afford."* In the film version *Cabaret*, Liza Minnelli as Sally Bowles declares gleefully, "These work instantly!"

(42)
See note (40)

(43)
See note (36)

(44)
Atlas Press, founded 1983, specialises in avant-garde writing from the 1890s to the present day. It is the largest publisher in English of books on Surrealism and has an extensive list relating to Dada, Surrealism, Expressionism, the Oulipo, the Collège de 'Pataphysique, the Vienna Actionists and others. *Oulipo*, short for French: *Ouvroir de littérature potentielle / Workshop of Potential Literature* is a loose gathering of (mainly) French-speaking writers and mathematicians who seek to create works using constrained writing techniques. It was founded in 1960 by Raymond Queneau and François Le Lionnais. Other notable members have included novelists Georges Perec and Italo Calvino, poets Oskar Pastior and Jean Lescure, and poet/mathematician Jacques Roubaud.

(45)
Teresa of Ávila (born Teresa Sánchez de Cepeda Dávila y Ahumada; 28 March 1515 – 4 or 15 October 1582) was a Carmelite nun, Spanish mystic and religious reformer. She is a principal character of the opera *Four Saints in Three Acts* (1934) by Virgil Thomson with a libretto by Gertrude Stein.

(46)

The Mother of Us All (1947) is a two-act opera composed by Virgil Thomson to a libretto by Gertrude Stein. The opera is about the life of Susan B. Anthony, one of the major figures in the struggle for women's suffrage in the United States. In the final aria, *All My Long Life*, Anthony, as a ghost, looks back over her life achievements: *We cannot retrace our steps, going forward may be the same as going backwards. We cannot retrace our steps, retrace our steps. All my long life, all my life, we do not retrace our steps, all my long life, but (A silence a long silence) But — we do not retrace our steps, all my long life, and here, here we are here, in marble and gold, did I say gold, yes I said gold, in marble and gold and where — (A silence) Where is where. In my long life of effort and strife, dear life, life is strife, in my long life, it will not come and go, I tell you so, it will stay it will pay but (A long silence) But do I want what we have got, has it not gone, what made it live, has it not gone because now it is had, in my long life in my long life (Silence) Life is strife, I was a martyr all my life not to what I won but to what was done. (Silence) Do you know because I tell you so, or do you know, do you know. (Silence) My long life, my long life.*

(47)
cf. V. *What the Thunder Said* from *The Waste Land* by
T.S. Eliot:
After the torchlight red on sweaty faces
After the frosty silence in the gardens
After the agony in stony places
The shouting and the crying

The wine drunk by the protagonists at lunch was
called *Stoney Vale*.